comets

Ricky and the Ram-Raiders

David Clayton

Illustrated by
Peter Dennis

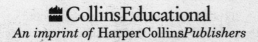
CollinsEducational
An imprint of HarperCollinsPublishers

Published by Collins Educational
77-85 Fulham Palace Road, London W6 8JB.

© HarperCollins*Publishers*

ISBN 0 00 323046 5

Reprinted 1996

Illustration and page layout by Peter Dennis
Cover design by Clinton Banbury
Cover illustration by Peter Dennis

Commissioning Editor: Domenica de Rosa
Editors: Rebecca Lloyd and Paula Hammond
Production: Mandy Inness

Typeset by Harper Phototypesetters Ltd.
Printed by HarperCollinsManufacturing Glasgow

Ricky and
the Ram-Raiders

Contents

To Ian McCarn,
the 'Flying Scotsman'.

Chapter 1 BLACK MONDAY

I love Mondays, don't you? Yeh, I love Mondays like vampires love sunbathing.

Take last Monday. Black sky, rain pinging off the windows, and something with sharp claws crawling over me. That was Useless, my one-eyed dog.

It was seven o'clock in the morning. The trouble was, waking up early gave me more time to think. I don't like thinking too much on Mondays.

It does my head in!

You see, Monday means P.E., and P.E. means BIG JOCK McLINTOCK - the games master.

Now, don't get me wrong - I love sport. Snooker, darts, Mortal Kombat, watching football...you name it, I play it, but...rugby?

McLintock is all rugby. I hate it, and Jock loves it. That's why the sparks fly when we meet.

And we meet first thing on Mondays.

Time to turn over and get some more zeds in. I rolled on to my face and...

Claws like Drac's fangs were spiking into my bottom!

So, up I got. Time to feed the mutt. Then the important bit - time to feed me! Double fried egg on toast. But...guess who ate the loaf while I was opening his tin?

Yes, I ended up with egg on egg.
Mum had already left for work. So, telly on and feet up. What was it to be - telly or Jock? No contest. TV won by a mile.

Five minutes later, we were off. By that time, I had a pair of sports socks on. I say a pair, well, only the colour bands were odd. It's near enough, isn't it?

As soon as the school came into view down the hill, one word popped into my head: McLintock!

What's the use of rugby anyway? But Danni is right. You can't duck out of everything, can you? Life isn't like that, is it?

Half-way down the hill, my mate Oxo popped up – stuffing himself as usual. This time his victim was a Mars bar. What a mouth! I've seen smaller car crushers.

When he'd finished munching and crunching and grunting he said one word:

Rugby!

I don't know why *he* hates Mondays. He's such a hippo, he should love rugby!

Laugh number one – assembly with Mr Pratt. He's the Head – Hillgate's answer to Horlicks.

Mind you, I don't mind his marathon prattle at all.

At least, not on Mondays. The more he goes on about everything, the less I have to put up with Jock's torture.

Mr Pratt was bouncing like a muppet. Today there was no shutting him up.

It was almost Christmas. But when I saw Jock at the end of my line, he looked as though Christmas had been called off in Scotland this year.

It was time to play games. My games.

Pratt was going on about school rules. I was getting ready for round one with Jock.

...children are leaving the school at dinnertime and going to the sweetshop...

Horrors! The sweetshop! Half the fifth-year bozos were ravers on 'E', and there he was going on about wine-gum abuse!

Oooo dear!

Mr Pratt leaned over.

His beaky nose cracked the mike.

DOINNNG!

Mr Punch's voice came out of the mob of kids, and they all laughed. I wonder who that could have been?

Pratt was giving us that 'we haff vays of making you talk!' routine he'd seen in old war films. But he hadn't got a clue the voice was me!

Jock had though! I could see his snake eyes shining as he closed in on me.

Smooth as a dinosaur.

Bad breath was curling the hair on my neck. I just stood quietly. Didn't even blink.

Unlucky Jock! You don't get me!

As soon as he'd turned to lumber back down the line, I started my song. It's amazing how loudly you can sing with your mouth shut.

Let the wind blow high,
Let the wind blow low,
Through the streets in ma kilt I'll go.
All the lassies say hallo,
Donald, where's yer troosers?

Jock had eyes like Darth Vader. He'd give me <u>Donald,</u> <u>Where's</u> <u>Yer</u> <u>Troosers</u> if he caught me. *If* Jockstrap! If dinosaurs could think!

Danielle was giving me the evil eye from the girls' line as they trooped out.

But Haggisheads don't bug me!

We left the hall.

Time for Lesson 1 – P.E.

We, the victims, stood alone. Jock stood – tall as a block of flats – at the top of the steps. His dark eyes ran down the line.

The No-Kit Black Book was in his hairy paws.

We were in *his* jungle now.

Jock's sausage finger was raised and he nailed me with his laser look.

9

Chapter 2 BIG JOCK

So there we were. Head to head.

Here!

Me and the Jockstrap.

I moved towards him. Fast enough to be doing what I was told. Slow enough to get to him. The game had started.

So, this is Richard Ryan: the well-known singer and comedian. Isn't that so, Mister Ryan?

It must be true if you say so, sir.

Very good of you to agree!

I gave him a little bow as if I was meeting the Queen or something. The lads got it right away. The laughs were starting.

Jock's voice was wobbling. I was winning on points already. But would he drop it? Get on with the lesson? No chance!

He had to have another go. Well, that was fine by me. The more you push, the worse I get.

How about a song now? How about singing <u>Donald</u> , <u>Where's Yer Troosers?</u>

How does it go, sir?

Is it:
<u>Let the wind blow high</u>,
<u>Let the wind blow low</u>,
<u>Through the streets in ma kilt I'll go</u>...?

Yes. That's the one.

Never heard of it!

You could have fried an egg on Jock's face.

You know, lads, poor wee Ryan here seems to be losing his memory. Perhaps he's a bit tapped in the head.

Tapped in the head? Doesn't that mean you think you're a teapot or Rambo or something, sir?

This brought a big roar. 'Rambo' was what the lads called McLintock. Everybody got the joke except Jock. Then bingo! He got it five seconds later.

11

I took a step back when I saw his eyes change. But I was lucky. Pratt came round the corner. He crashed into a waste bin, stared at Jock as if it was his fault, then scuttled off. Now Mister Magoo was gone, Jock could come out to play again.

I'm tired o' you, son! You can have a private rugby lesson wi' me at four o'clock, okay?

Right, you deadbeats, into the changing rooms and get your kit on. Two minutes! I'll get the rugby balls.

'Ah'm Jock-Raambo! Eat dirt, you suckers!'

So into the gas chamber we went. Stinky socks were everywhere! It was quiet for ten seconds, then:

The class were laughing their socks off. I didn't hear McLintock until the bag of rugby balls hit me on the head.

Do us Jock-Rambo, Ricky!

My favourite act!

THUNK!

Four o'clock, Ryan. Make my day!

Chapter 3 BLOOD MATCH

Out we went, slipping and slopping and sliding across the boggy field.

McLintock is a nutter. Rugby is a game for loonies. To make it worse, Danni and her mob were playing football. That's really rubbing it in, isn't it?

Jock was talking to Birch, a big rugby player with two bellies, the captain of my team.
Trouble? They kept looking over at me and grinning.
I knew what they wanted. Me to have a free holiday in casualty!

No chance, headbangers! Catch me if you can!

I went out on the wing. That is, as far from the ball and the other team as possible. Out there, I wouldn't hurt them. More important, they couldn't hurt me. Oxo was marking me. We'd fixed it like that.

Jock had a face like a wet Sunday in Glasgow. He couldn't *make* them give me the ball! I'd escaped! Or so I thought...

I had a quick look at what Danni was doing. There she was, up front, a striker! And here I was, playing pass the parcel with Jock. Great!

A jet came singing over. It was a silver speck against the blue sky. And, suddenly, my mind was up there with those people. They were heading south, to Spain or Italy.
Spain - Barcelona!
Italy - A.C. Milan!
I often watch planes. Think of being on them
...being signed for 15 million like Ryan Giggs...

15

There was no hiding place in the scrum. The hard faces and bodies were waiting for me. Their *boots* weighed more than me! It all looked like bad news, and I was not wrong.

First scrum down, a big fist crashed into my ribs.

Electric sparks ran all over me. Nobody saw anything.

I knew who it was – Birch! One of *ours*! Jock's eyes were shining black marbles. Time for <u>The</u> <u>Great</u> <u>Escape.</u>

Get on with it, lads!

HA! HA! HA!

Birch, sort it out!

HA! HA!

But Birch couldn't look at Jock.

17

Jock had taken one step towards me when a voice cut into him from the touch line.

Is there some trouble, Mr McLintock?

Good old Mr Pratt! I'll never take the mickey out of him again! There he was in his curly coat and Russian hat. My hero!

I started to limp off like Quasimodo before Jock could dish the dirt on me.

I'm hurt, sir.

McLintock had to take it all like Mister Nice Guy, didn't he?

Danielle's game finished before ours.

Well, I told you!

I know!

I thought about the plane I had seen earlier. Maybe I should get one. To Australia!

Chapter 4 RUNAWAY

I didn't hang around in the changing rooms to wish Jock a happy dinner time. I legged it to the yard as soon as I got changed.

Ten minutes later, Oxo came up, looking as though someone had died.

You're dead! He had a go at me just for being your mate!

Are you trying to cheer me up or what?

There was no way *now* that I was going to let McLintock make a meal of me at four o'clock. But there was a problem. You know already that Danielle doesn't like me running away. But do I really have to take life on the chin all the time? I don't think so.

Coming to the canteen?

No, got to feed Useless. Got to go home.

No bunking off!

Would I do that?

She gave me *that* look she has. Then she turned and walked away without a word.

As soon as she was out of sight, I was legging it down the hill *away* from home.

Soon, I was clear of the school. Why did the air taste so sweet, even though my ribs hurt? Because it was free air, not school air!

Now time for dinner. I dipped in my pockets and – bingo! Enough for a burger and fries.

Loved it, and only splattered a bit of sauce on my jeans. Well, nobody's perfect, are they?

Then it was red-hot coffee. Better than the school dishwater, eh?

What now? Home?
No, Mum might catch me. The arcades?
What with? Washers? Chocolate buttons?
The old factory? No, boring on your own.
The river park and the tree house? Yes, brilliant!
No teachers or council truant men to catch you
down there! Even Danni doesn't know it.
So, afternoon fun here we come!

Soon I was clear of the town. The pathways followed the foamy river. Sometimes they were wide. Sometimes they were narrow. Some came to a dead end, while others were as wide as a street. It was wet and messy.

The tree house was three miles in, and well hidden. I didn't make it. Halfway there, on a path we call the Devil's Highway, I could hear an engine thundering. All sorts of people use the park. Sometimes you don't want to meet them. Sometimes they don't want to meet you.

I hid behind a tree. You can't be too careful. Too many weirdos knocking about these days.

What was going on? I was so amazed that I stepped out to watch it. That was a mistake – a big mistake!

It was flying again.
But, this time, it was heading for me!
I was legging it like mad for a gap in the trees.

Then I was off. Faster than Linford Christie. I had one look back. A figure in black was staring down the track. Just eyes showing!

You're dead!

I wish people would stop saying that!

My heart was bouncing off my ribs like a basketball. My breath was chugging like a steam train.

T! UFF! PUFF! PANT!

I couldn't run any more. The wood was quiet, too quiet. Tall, bare trees made a zig-zag of purple shadows. The river slid by, dark and shiny and deep. But no men popped up. I was alone.

Soon I was back in the park. Then, I was out on the road.

What now? School? Jock? No chance!

I was still thinking as a van came up behind me.

I caught a glimpse of it out of the corner of my eye.

YAAAAA!

Want a lift?

It was too late. No escape!

Oxo's tomato face popped up at the window.

Come on, Ricky. You'll be late for school!

Don't do that!

Wrong van. No escape. School and Jock.

26

Chapter 5 GOTCHA!

So there I was – back at school. Good old Oxo – I *don't* think! Two seconds after I went through the gate, guess who arrived? Yes, Danielle.

Where've you been? I rang your house.

Thinking.

Thinking of bunking off?

I said nothing and was just about to go in when Wayne Taylor, a fifth-year scumball, waved me over to a side door.

You been out this dinner?

What's it to you?

You been down Riverside?

Danielle saw my look and didn't ask any more. It was going to be a long day. But I didn't know just how long!

Last lesson came too soon. It was a library period. And guess who turned up there? Yes, Superjock himself. Imagine – all he reads is the <u>Beano</u> and there he was, near all those books. He was dying to get at me.

A big shadow fell across my book.

Here goes.

I was not wrong. But he was a mug to try to get to me.

What are you reading, son?

That figures. The 'wonderland' suits you. And the 'Alice' maybe.

<u>Alice</u> in <u>Wonderland</u>, sir. It's all about weird people.

Then Mr Brown came zooming across the room.

He gave Jock the evil eye. It was bad enough having noisy kids in his library. He didn't want noisy teachers as well. Jock went red. Now people were laughing at *him*.

I felt like a sack of rubbish as Jock zipped away to check. The books were there. I knew. I'd set it up!

Now Mr Brown was part of our game. He and Jock were eyeball to eyeball.

Not in here, Mr McLintock!

Jock rushed outside. Just outside. The bell went.

Right, out you go. All except you, Ryan.

The name hit me like a wet fish. He never called me 'Ryan'. Never, ever.
I could see a big shadow outside the door.

The librarian said nothing at first but shook his head. The silence was worse than a telling-off.

Ricky, you have gone too far this time!

At least I'm Ricky now.

He hates me.

Will he like you better this way? Life's hard enough without making enemies. He's a proud man. Thinks only about you kids since his wife died. But he can't bear to lose. He can't lose any more.

Yes, sir.

Give him more respect.

Yes, sir.

Are you listening, Ricky?

Yes, sir.

Hmmmmm. Go.

Use your brain a bit more.

Yes, sir.

I opened the door and found - just what I expected.

Good evening, Songbird! Welcome to my world!

Chapter 6 THE MUSIC MAN

The walk to the gym was like going to the hangman.

You're dead! You're dead!

When I got there, guess what? Danielle was waiting there, hanging about. Jock's dark eyes were on her. He wasn't daft either.

Can I help you, young lady?

No, sir. I'm waiting for Miss Foster.

Well, well, well! Danni telling lies! Everyone knew that Miss Foster was off sick. Even the caretaker's cat knew that! Jock's face looked harder than ever.

Then Oxo came lumbering up. At one second past four he was usually belting home for tea. Wild horses couldn't get between him and his chips! And here he was at the gym!

Can I help you to pump up the balls, sir?

No, son.

Fantastic! Oxo helping Mr McLintock! Jock's face would have scared crows away. No rough stuff now. Not with two witnesses! Crafty devils!

But the lesson would go on. As I changed alone the door boomed open. Jock strode in with a chair and a piece of chalk. He marked a cross on the floor. What was he up to?

Stand there.

He was mad, potty.

Wait.

What now? Were we digging for treasure? Had Jockstrap hidden the McLintock family gold under the floor?

Was it the haggis-growing season? Or a tunnel to Jock's whisky store?

Sing!

This was a funny rugby lesson!

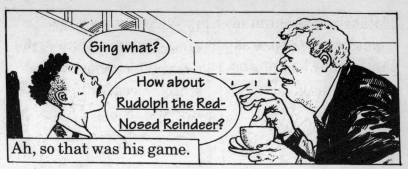

Ah, so that was his game.

I was away. But as soon as the song was over –

Jock's eyes were like bullets.

It was very cold in the changing room. I decided to warm myself up.

This time, I jumped about as if I was giving a concert at Wembley or something. After I had sung the song ten times, Jock was fed up. He had no tea left, no biscuits. He was cold, and *I* looked as if I was enjoying myself.

He was just about to say 'again' when there was this terrible banging on the door.

BANG! BANG! BANG! BANG!

Mr McLintock!

It was Mrs Ferret, the music teacher. She was the Great White Shark of the school. Even Mr Pratt was scared of her.

Mr McLintock!

There was *death* in her voice.

I understand that this boy has been singing <u>Rudolph the Red-Nosed Reindeer</u> for half an hour.

He thinks he's a singer...

He is a singer. A very good singer. Singing is not a punishment...and if you're too stupid to understand that....

Ouch! I could feel the words hitting him.

I wonder who told her about the singing? Couldn't have been Danielle by any chance!

Round one to you, son. But you don't beat me. Oh, no!

Uh, oh! Goodbye sweet world!

Now...the rugby lesson!

Chapter 7 NOW THE RUGBY LESSON

In a few seconds, Jock had taken off his tracksuit. Now, he was down to his rugby kit. His size-fourteen boots looked like coal barges. Hair stood up on my neck. It was not going to be a fitness lesson. It was going to be an injury lesson. A pain lesson. My pain.

It was growing dark. Mist came across from the moor. The trees at the end of the field were like ghostly soldiers. I'd be a ghost myself if I didn't
watch it.

No use telling Jock jokes.
Only one way to beat him.

And we did. Run twenty metres, walk back. Twenty metres, walk back. On and on. But I'll give him this – he ran too.

Now I knew how to get to him. I'd wear him down. I can run. Five runs. Ten runs. My breath was singing and so was his! Fifteen runs!

He looked at me.

But he was shaking his head.

Chapter 7 NOW THE RUGBY LESSON

In a few seconds, Jock had taken off his tracksuit. Now, he was down to his rugby kit. His size-fourteen boots looked like coal barges. Hair stood up on my neck. It was not going to be a fitness lesson. It was going to be an injury lesson. A pain lesson. My pain.

It was growing dark. Mist came
across from the moor. The trees at
the end of the field were like ghostly
soldiers. I'd be a ghost myself if I
didn't
watch it.

No use telling Jock jokes.
Only one way to beat him.

And we did. Run twenty metres, walk back. Twenty
metres, walk back. On and on. But I'll give him this
– he ran too.

Now I knew how to get to him. I'd wear him down. I
can run. Five runs. Ten runs. My breath was singing
and so was his! Fifteen runs!

He looked at me.

But he was shaking his head.

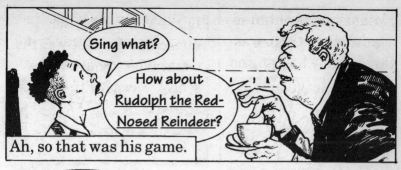

Ah, so that was his game.

I was away. But as soon as the song was over –

Sing it again.

Jock's eyes were like bullets.

It was very cold in the changing room. I decided to warm myself up.

This time, I jumped about as if I was giving a concert at Wembley or something. After I had sung the song ten times, Jock was fed up. He had no tea left, no biscuits. He was cold, and *I* looked as if I was enjoying myself.

He was just about to say 'again' when there was this terrible banging on the door.

BANG! BANG! BANG! BANG!

Mr McLintock!

It was Mrs Ferret, the music teacher. She was the Great White Shark of the school. Even Mr Pratt was scared of her.

Mr McLintock!

There was *death* in her voice.

I understand that this boy has been singing <u>Rudolph the Red-Nosed Reindeer</u> for half an hour.

He thinks he's a singer...

He is a singer. A very good singer. Singing is not a punishment...and if you're too stupid to understand that....

Ouch! I could feel the words hitting him.

I wonder who told her about the singing? Couldn't have been Danielle by any chance!

Round one to you, son. But you don't beat me. Oh, no!

Uh, oh! Goodbye sweet world!

Now...the rugby lesson!

38

And I was away, splatting, splashing, flopping, rolling. Jock crunched along, bogged down by his big body. Half-way and I was winning! Then the pain came. My lungs were on fire. His big boots came closer and closer. My boots got boggier and boggier.

His breath was like broken bagpipes.
A block of concrete seemed to rest on my chest.

Five metres before the line he came by.

We flopped down almost together. Now, we were just two heaps of mud. All I could see were his eyes.

But did I see...a little grin? From Jock?

The lesson must be over. Just *had* to be.

One more thing
– the tackle.

The tackle?
I'm dead!

I had a quick look round in the gloom. Two shadowy shapes, one tall and leggy, one square and eating, showed through the mist. My friends were still around.

But people just 'get hurt' in rugby, don't they? It's that sort of sport, isn't it?

Run at me. I'll take you above the knee.

Great! What would he do then? Sellotape me back together again? Dig me out of the mud with a JCB?

But it didn't work out like that. I ran like hell. He bumped me in just the right place. My rubber legs were going nowhere.

SPLAT!

Again.

Again?

He hit me neat and clean ten times. Each time I got a faceful of mud.

No. Now you knock me down.

Here it comes!

WAAAA!

The Flying Scotsman had run me over. Another mud mouthwash!

43

Here! You can take anyone like that. And these days you never know when you might have to. AGAIN!

By now it was so dark, I could hardly see his face. But I could see that he was grinning.

Now he'd get his own back for all the jokes and songs. Now he'd crush me flat for sure.

In he came, faster, just as I thought, and...

This time he was really running hard. Shoulder down, wait, wait, then –

WHAM!

ZZAP!!

He was on the floor!

Again!

Down he went like a bag of spuds.

We both sat like babies in a sand pit.

I was free! Or so I thought.
I'd forgotten about the man in the mask!

Chapter 8 FUNNY FEELINGS

Do you ever get funny feelings? A feeling that something is going to happen but you don't know what?

Well, I felt like that when I walked off that field. Jock was being nice enough. It wasn't him.

No, there was something in the air. Something about the shadows.

I pulled Danni close to me.

How can you be cold after all that running about?

She didn't get it. I wasn't cold, but I was shivering. My mind was back in the woods. Back with the blue van. Back in the yard with Wayne. I could hear his voice: 'Call an ambulance...'.

I turned to her. Looked at her chestnut hair and green eyes. I didn't want her to get hurt. I was about to say something about what was going on when suddenly, Oxo cut in, chattering on about nothing as usual.

Give it a rest, Oxo.

All right. Goodnight, then.

He was gobbled up by the mist as we went different ways.

After a minute I remembered that I hadn't thanked him for keeping an eye on Jock.

Thanks for stopping behind!

I should have thanked him before.

Yes. You should have, but you didn't.

I'd heard this song before. Was I always thinking about myself?

47

Chapter 9 THE LUCK OF THE DRAW

We were on our way out. Then I had a real bit of luck.

Hey!

Yes?

So what?

Help me, and I'll give you half the winnings.

Can you work this machine? I've got four nudges and I'm running out of time.

Easy-peasy!

Right, we're leaving...

Just one game...

CLICK! CLICK! CLICK! CLICK! BINGO!

Now, Ricky! It's a mug's game. I'm off!

Suddenly I had seven quid in ten pences in my pocket.

So out we went. My pockets were down to my knees!

Out in the dark side street we ran smack into Wayne's mob, but no Wayne.

We've been watching you. Big winner, eh? Let's have it then!

Okay, we'll take it, then.

I don't think so.

Here you are, then, Pizza-face! Help yourself!

The coins flew like sparks in the light of the streetlamps.

ARRR! I'm blind!

Run!

Danni didn't need telling twice.

It was always her buying stuff for me, what with her Dad giving her loads of spends and my Mum getting peanuts at the bakery. But I don't mind too much. She's all right, my Mum. When she's not mad at me for being so messy. Anyway, now it was burger time! But, right then, Wayne and his brother Shark were making plans, violent plans. Anybody who got in their way was going to suffer. But it didn't spoil my tea. I didn't know about it, did I?

Chapter 10 THE CRUNCH

The warm air in the burger bar hit you smack in the face. And the tinny Christmas music hammered your ears. The place was all full of kids with shiny faces.

Why don't you get something big to eat? I can still see your hair over the top of it!

Har, har, har! Did Oxo tell you that one?

Did you see that?

What?

Wayne Taylor.

Where?

Outside the window.

She took one step forward before I heard *the sound*. It was coming closer — fast. *Very fast!*

Litter bins flew aside. Benches splintered. On and on and on the van came, the Christmas lights sparkling in its dark windows.

Then Wayne was off, like a sprinter from the blocks.

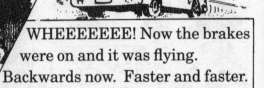

WHEEEEEEE! Now the brakes were on and it was flying. Backwards now. Faster and faster.

The jeweller's! Winter's!

SMASH!

SCREECH!

And into the window it went. People were running like chickens with no heads. Wayne was on his way with a big bag. Now he had a mask on! The ram-raid was on.

Danielle was on her way.

Come on!

But she was in like a Rottweiler, grabbing Wayne and pinning his arms. Two other men were in the shop, piling the jewellery into bags.

Hang on, they might have a gun.

I can't move! The girl's got me!

Get in!

The shop alarm was clanging loud enough to wake the dead.

Still I held off. *Did* they have a shotgun? You don't get a second chance with them. They take your head off. The estate's full of them. That's why Danni stormed in and I didn't. She doesn't know about stuff like that. I do!

Suddenly, the two big men in balaclavas jumped out and dragged Wayne into the van with Danni still hanging on to him!

They were getting away! They'd got her. Got Danni. Gun or no gun, I went charging in! Running like mad.

Luckily, the van slowed to get round the giant Christmas tree. In I dived, right through the driver's open window and grabbed the wheel.

Get off! I can't...

KERRUNCH!

THUNK!

It was all falling jam-side down for them now. No driver. No fast van!

Let's get out of here!

The crowd stood and watched. Just *watched*! I ask you! Wimps! The three ram-raiders were getting away!

Stop them!

Nobody moved! But you should have seen Danielle run. And she did karate.

She took out Wayne neat as anything. His nose didn't bounce very well on the pavement.

Those words again! *Him!*

I took him just above the knee! His head hit the concrete like a coconut.

Shame about the third one. There he was – a big, powerful, hard case – way down the precinct with his hold-all, legging it like mad.

Then, something came flying out of a sports shop.

CRUNCH!

WOW! What a hit! You could hear the crunch from here to China as that ram-raider bit the dust. I'd know a McLintock tackle anywhere!

It was finished. Jewellery was scattered all over the place. The police snapped up three of the robbers. The fourth went by ambulance.

The jewellers were all over us. Dead chuffed with us all, especially wonderwoman Danielle! And Big Jock was grinning like a lighthouse.

59

When it was all sorted out, we went back to the burger bar to start all over again. Jock joined us.